W9-CNW-805

Parents and Caregivers,

Stone Arch Readers are designed to provide enjoyable reading experiences, as well as opportunities to develop vocabulary, literacy skills, and comprehension. Here are a few ways to support your beginning reader:

- Talk with your child about the ideas addressed in the story.

- Discuss each illustration, mentioning the characters, where they are, and what they are doing.

- Read with expression, pointing to each word. You may want to read the whole story through and then revisit parts of the story to ensure that the meanings of words or phrases are understood.

- Talk about why the character did what he or she did and what your child would do in that situation.

- Help your child connect with characters and events in the story.

Remember, reading with your child should be fun, not forced. Each moment spent reading with your child is a priceless investment in his or her literacy life.

Gail Saunders-Smith, Ph.D.

STONE ARCH READERS

are published by Stone Arch Books
A Capstone Imprint
151 Good Counsel Drive, P.O. Box 669
Mankato, Minnesota 56002
www.capstonepub.com

Library of Congress Cataloging-in-Publication Data
    Meister, Cari.
    The fancy octopus / by Cari Meister; illustrated by Steve Harpster.
    p. cm. — (Stone Arch readers. Ocean tales)
    Summary: Margo the octopus is worried about being a model in an upcoming
fashion show because when she gets nervous she squirts ink.
    ISBN 978-1-4342-3201-4 (library binding)
    ISBN 978-1-4342-3392-9 (pbk.)
    [1. Octopuses—Fiction. 2. Fashion shows—Fiction. 3. Self-confidence—Fiction.]
I. Harpster, Steve, ill. II. Title.
PZ7.M515916Fan 2011
[E]—dc22

                        2011000298

                Art Director: Kay Fraser
                Designer: Emily Harris
            Production Specialist: Michelle Biedscheid

                Reading Consultants:

                Gail Saunders-Smith, Ph.D.
                Melinda Melton Crow, M.Ed.
            Laurie K. Holland, Media Specialist

        Printed in the United States of America in Melrose Park, Illinois.
                        032011
                    006112LKF11

The Fancy Octopus

by Cari Meister

illustrated by Steve Harpster

STONE ARCH BOOKS
a capstone imprint

Margo
the Octopus

OCTOPUS FUN FACTS

- An octopus can squeeze its body through a hole the size of its own eyeball.

- An octopus can change the color, pattern, and feel of its skin to blend in and hide.

- An octopus can lay as many as 100,000 eggs at a time. Each egg is about the size of a grain of rice.

- A newborn octopus's length is equal to the width of two quarters stacked on top of each other — just one-eighth of an inch.

Margo and Claire lived deep in the sea. They did everything together.

They went to the movies.

They played games.

They had sleepovers.

One day, Margo and Claire
saw a poster.

"Let's go!" said Claire. "It sounds so fancy."

"I'm not sure," said Margo.

"Why not?" asked Claire.

Before Margo could answer,
she squirted some black ink.

"When I feel nervous, I squirt
ink," she said.

Claire felt bad for her friend. But she wanted to be in the fashion show.

"Please try," said Claire. "I know you would be great!"

"Okay, I'll try," said Margo. "It does sound like fun."

On Saturday morning, the friends met at the Shell Walk. Fish rushed past them carrying gowns.

"Everything's so fancy!" said Margo.

"Look!" Claire said. "There's Ms. Dotty!"

Ms. Dotty was very fancy.

She walked with style.

She talked with style.

She even laughed with style.

Ms. Dotty made Margo nervous. Margo squirted a little ink.

"Oops," she said. "I hope no one saw that."

"I did," said Claire. "But I won't tell anyone. Here, use my scarf."

"Thanks!" said Margo. "You are the best."

Ms. Dotty gathered the girls.

"The show is in one week," said Ms. Dotty. "Today we will choose your gowns. Then we will practice."

Ms. Dotty pointed to a long walkway. "You will go to the end of the Shell Walk," she said. "When I ring the bell, swim toward me."

The girls formed a line. A sea horse handed Claire a red gown and a crown. He gave Margo a blue gown with a sash.

"Don't ruin anything," he said. "I want everything back in perfect shape!"

The girls went into the
dressing room and got dressed.
"We look so fancy!" said Claire.

"I don't feel very fancy," said
Margo.

Claire smiled at her friend. "Try not to be nervous. If you squirt ink, you might ruin the clothes," she said.

That made Margo even more nervous.

Ms. Dotty rang the bell.
Claire went first.

She swam down the Shell
Walk with her nose high in the
air. She looked beautiful.

Margo was next. She was so
nervous she could hardly move.
Her arms were stiff and straight.

Then, Margo squirted!

Ms. Dotty looked surprised.
Margo was sure she would be
asked to leave.

Ms. Dotty started clapping. "What a fancy octopus!" she said.

"Me? Fancy?" asked Margo. "But what about my squirting?"

"It gives you an air of mystery, my dear," said Ms. Dotty.

"But there is one thing," said Ms. Dotty. "You shouldn't be modeling a dress."

"I shouldn't?" Margo asked.

"No," said Ms. Dotty, "a girl with your arms belongs in jewelry."

And in the end, Margo truly was fancy.

The End